To my mother, Eva, the sweetest Swede I know — A.D.

To my lovely Magda, for our 25th best-friend-iversary — L.J.S.

Kids Can Press acknowledges the financial support of the Government of
Ontario, through the Ontario Media Development Corporation's Ontario
Book Initiative; the Ontario Arts Council; the Canada Council for the Arts;
and the Government of Canada, through the CBF, for our publishing activity.

Published in Canada by
Kids Can Press Ltd.
25 Dockside Drive
Toronto, ON M5A 0B5

Published in the U.S. by
Kids Can Press Ltd.
2250 Military Road
Tonawanda, NY 14150

www.kidscanpress.com

The artwork in this book was rendered in pencil and colored in Photoshop.
The text is set in Garamond and Clue.

Edited by Yvette Ghione
Designed by Karen Powers

This book is smyth sewn casebound.
Manufactured in Shenzhen, China, in 11/2014 by C & C Offset

CM 15 0 9 8 7 6 5 4 3 2 1

Library and Archives Canada Cataloguing in Publication

Dunklee, Annika, 1965–, author

   Me, too! / written by Annika Dunklee ; illustrated by

Lori Joy Smith.

ISBN 978-1-77138-104-8 (bound)

   I. Smith, Lori Joy, 1973–, illustrator II. Title.

PS8607.U542M4 2015   jC813'.6   C2014-902895-4

Kids Can Press is a *Corus*™ Entertainment company

Me, Too!

Written by Annika Dunklee

Illustrated by Lori Joy Smith

Kids Can Press

This is Annie.

And this is her best friend, Lillemor.
She's from Sweden.
    They are best friends for many reasons.

Reason # 1

They're the same age.

Reason # 2

They like the same colors.

Reason # 3

They like doing the same things.

And most important …

Reason # 4

They can both speak another language.

Okay, so Annie made hers up,
but she is pretty sure it still counts.

When Annie goes to Lillemor's house, she
gets to try all different kinds of Swedish foods.

And when Lillemor goes to Annie's house,
Annie likes her to try something different, too.

Sometimes they even try on each other's clothes.

They are the best of friends.

Every day when Annie arrives at school,
Lillemor greets her with a big hug.

But one day when Annie arrives at school,
there is no Lillemor. And no big hug.

Where could she be?

Annie looks high and low
in the schoolyard for Lillemor.
And, sure enough, there she is …
playing with somebody else?!

Lillemor and another girl are jumping rope.
They are having fun. AND they are laughing!
Annie doesn't like the look of this at all.

Annie frowns. Both girls' names begin with "Lil"!
*Lil*ianne. *Lil*lemor.
Annie doesn't have a single "L" in her name!

Lilianne can speak another language, too?
Annie is not happy about this at all.

(Now she is a little less sure that Oinky Boinky counts.)

Annie decides she needs to ask Lilianne
some VERY important questions.

Question #1

So, Lilianne,
what are YOUR
favorite colors?

I LOVE
rose and
violette!

Annie is relieved.
For a moment.

Question # 2

Lilianne, how old are you?

I am SIX.

Finally! Something Lilianne and Lillemor do NOT have in common.

Or so Annie thinks.

Annie can't stand it.

* I can't stand it!

She pulls her hood over her head.

What's wrong, Annie?
You two have so many things in common! I'm feeling left out!
Left out?!

Annie giggles.

I like jumping rope, pink and purple and speaking another language, too!

I know!

And you and I both have "Ann" in our names! Lili*Anne*. *Ann*ie.

This is music to Annie's ears.

Wow! We ALL have so many things in common!

And we can ALL play together!

YES, we do!

YES, we can!

Annie is SO relieved.

Annie has just one last, very important question to ask Lilianne.

This is Annie, Lillemor AND Lilianne.
They are best friends for many reasons ...

✳ Of course!   ✳ Absolutely!   ✱ Definitely!